Disney's

Doug's™
SECRET
CHRISTMAS

Created by
Jim Jinkins

JUMBO
PICTURES
INC.

GRADE **A** QUALITY

Original script by Ken Scarborough • Adapted by Jan Carr

Illustrated by Matthew C. Peters • Tim Chi Ly • Alisa Klayman • Cheng-li Chan • Tony Curanaj • Brian Donnelly

DISNEY
PRESS

NEW YORK

Disney's
DouG's
SECRET
CHRISTMAS

'Twas the week before Christmas, and all through Bluffington folks were caught up in the holiday spirit. They crowded into Bullseye Park to watch the mayor light the town tree.

In the yard next to the Funnies, Mr. Dink tinkered with his Santa display.

"Hubba, hubba!" chuckled Santa.
"No!" shouted Mr. Dink. "It's 'Ho, ho, ho'!"

Doug couldn't wait to decorate the family tree and help his father string lights outside. On Christmas Eve, they'd visit Grandma Funnie, and there'd be piles of fruitcake and plenty of presents.

But first, Doug had to write his list.
"Whaddya think . . . in-line skates or a dirt bike?" he asked.
Porkchop shrugged.
"You're right, Porkchop. Both." Doug raced downstairs with his list in hand.

Doug's mom was resting on the couch because she was pregnant. Very pregnant. And getting bigger by the day.

"Son," said his dad, "with the baby coming, Santa's not going to have a lot of time for presents this year."

"Sure, Dad," stammered Doug. He hid the list behind his back. "I was just writing a list of . . . baby names."

Judy snatched the list out of his hands. "Dirt bike?" she laughed. "Oh, that's a *perfect* name for a baby. Personally, I prefer Cleopatra."

The next day, on the way home from school, Doug stopped at the lot where Mr. Chestnut was selling Christmas trees. He breathed in his favorite holiday smell, the scent of freshly cut pine.

"Well, look who's here!" cried Mr. Chestnut. "My best customer!"

"I'll come back later with my dad," Doug promised.

Doug imagined how fun it was going to be to decorate the tree.

But when Doug got home, his dad already had a tree, and it definitely wasn't what he was expecting. It was a puny artificial tree.

"We don't have time for a real tree this year," said his dad. "Not with the baby coming."

Doug's mom and dad put on their coats and hustled out the door to go to birth buddy class.

"Merry Christmas," Doug said sadly.

A few days before Christmas, Doug and Skeeter went to the mall. Doug wanted to get just the right present for Patti. Finally he found the perfect pair of earrings. He counted out his money. Just enough!

"Hey, Doug!" called Skeeter. Skeeter wanted to buy a Christmas-tree–shaped waffle iron for his dad but it was way too much money.

"How much do you need?" asked Doug. He gave Skeeter the money from his wallet. That left Doug with sixty-three cents.

Finally it was Christmas Eve, and Doug still had to get a present for Patti.

"I know!" he cried. "I'll make her a pair of earrings myself!"

Doug mixed flour, salt, and water and molded tiny earrings. He ran to Patti's house to give her the present.

"They're great!" she cried as she held up the earrings.

Patti gave Doug a present, too. "But don't open it till Christmas," she instructed.

Doug's Secret Recipe
(for bread dough earrings or ornaments)

2 cups of flour
1 cup of salt
1 cup of water
wire
acrylic paint
earring loops from craft store

- Mix flour, salt, and water together. Knead the dough until smooth. Roll the dough 1/8-inch thick on a floured board.
- Using cookie cutters or patterns you've traced on cardboard, cut dough into your favorite shapes.
  Decorate with strips or beads of dough. Bend a 3/4-inch length of wire into a U-shape and insert for hanging.
- Bake dough shapes on a cookie sheet at 200 degrees for 8 hours (with a parent's supervision) or until dry.
  When the dough cools, paint with acrylic paint.
- Attach earring loops.

All the way home, Doug wished for the kind of Christmas he'd seen on TV. He imagined a snowy winter scene. Sequined skaters were spinning on the ice and Chap Lipman was singing "The More You Give, the More You Get."

But Doug knew he wouldn't have the Christmas of his dreams. Mr. Dink's Santa was chanting, "Blah, blah, blah," and Doug's dad hadn't even bothered to hang any lights.

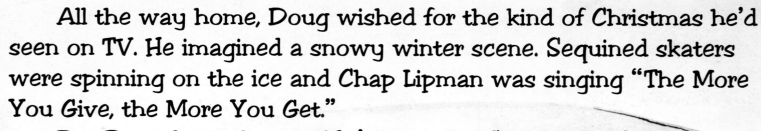

"What time are we going to Grandma Funnie's?" Doug asked his mom.

"I'm afraid we won't be going," she told him. "Not this year."

Doug went to his room and threw himself across his bed. No lights. No tree. What an awful Christmas!

"We can't let this happen!" he vowed. "Come on, Porkchop!"

Doug ran out of the house and headed for Mr. Chestnut's Christmas tree lot.

Mr. Chestnut was already packing up. He pulled a small tree down from the truck. "I think I have one just for you," he said. "Merry Christmas, son. "

Doug tucked the tree under his arm and headed home. He was determined to have a good Christmas. Even if he had to make his own, *secret* Christmas.

Doug and Porkchop set up the tree in Doug's room. Together they trimmed it with their favorite things.

On Christmas morning, Doug opened his journal. "Dear Journal: Merry Christmas," he wrote. Porkchop handed him a present— a brand new journal for a brand new year! Doug gave Porkchop a mug.

Then Doug realized the house was very quiet. Doug peered into his parents' room. Empty. He pounded on Judy's door. Where was everybody?

"Mom!" he called. "Dad! Judy!" His voice echoed eerily through the house.

Just then, the phone rang. It was his dad.

"We're at the hospital," he explained. "In all the confusion, I guess we sort of ran out and left you. Sorry—I'm on my way."

Doug's dad picked him up and drove him to the hospital. As he was rushed into the room, Doug wasn't sure what to expect.

"Meet your new baby sister," said his mom. In her arms she held a sweet baby girl.

"We decided to use the names you and Judy came up with," said his dad.

"Meet Cleopatra Dirtbike Funnie," their mother said.

The Funnie family finally celebrated Christmas two days later. But it really didn't matter *when* Christmas happened. It was more like a feeling—a special feeling about friends, family, and especially a new baby sister.

"Hey, Doug," said Patti. "Aren't you going to open my present?"
Doug's present was a scarf. One end was fat and one was thin.
"I ran out of yarn," Patti giggled. She gave her friend a quick hug.
"Merry Christmas," she said.

Doug wrapped the scarf around his neck and ran outside to buy diapers for his new baby sister. Mr. Dink was packing up his Santa display. "Ho, ho, ho!" Santa chuckled, at last.

"Merry Christmas, everybody!" shouted Doug.